Leveling Up

Deborah Zoe Laufer

D0932947

A SAMUEL FRENCH ACTING EDITION

FOUNDED 1830

SAMUELFRENCH.COM
SAMUELFRENCH-LONDON.CO.UK

FOR PRODUCTION ENQUIRIES

UNITED STATES AND CANADA
Info@SamuelFrench.com
1-866-598-8449

UNITED KINGDOM AND EUROPE
Plays@SamuelFrench-London.co.uk
020-7255-4302

Each title is subject to availability from Samuel French, depending upon country of performance. Please be aware that *LEVELING UP* may not be licensed by Samuel French in your territory. Professional and amateur producers should contact the nearest Samuel French office or licensing partner to verify availability.

MUSIC USE NOTE

IMPORTANT BILLING AND CREDIT REQUIREMENTS

LEVELING UP was first produced by the Cincinnati Playhouse in the Park at the Thompson Shelterhouse in Cincinnati, Ohio on February 9, 2013. The performance was directed by Wendy C. Goldberg, with sets by Kevin Depinet, costumes by Anne Kennedy, lights by Josh Epstein, and sound by Benji Inniger. The Production Stage Manager was Becky Merold. The cast was as follows:

JEANNIE . . . . Ali Rose Dachis

IAN . . . . Sean Mellott

CHUCK . . . . Bobby Moreno

ZANDER. . . . . Ben Morrow

LEVELING UP was subsequently produced by Steppenwolf for Young Adults in Chicago, IL on February 26, 2014. The performance was directed by Hallie Gordon, with sets and costumes by Brian Bembridge, lights by J.R. Lederle, and sound by Rick Sims. The Production Stage Manager was Jonathan Nook. The cast was as follows:

JEANNIE . . . . Carolyn Braver

IAN . . . . Clancy McCartney

CHUCK . . . . Jerry MacKinnon

ZANDER . . . . JJ Phillips

Development of *LEVELING UP* was supported by the Eugene O'Neill Theater Center during a residency at the National Playwrights Conference, 2011 (Preston Whiteway, Executive Director; Wendy Goldberg, Artistic Director).

CHARACTERS

IAN – Early 20's. Awesome gamer: Nevada State champ. A bit of a nerd. Very bright.

CHUCK – Ian's roommate. Early 20's. All around good guy.

ZANDER – Ian's other roommate. Early 20's. Very good looking. A bit of a wheeler dealer.

JEANNIE – Zan's girlfriend. Very sweet and innocent. Excellent student. 21

SETTING

All action takes place in Ian, Chuck, and Zan's basement game room, save Scene 8, when we see Ian at work.

TIME

2011

AUTHOR'S NOTES

The play is played in 10 scenes without an intermission.

A slash / in a line indicates overlaping dialogue.

For Charlie and Alex

Scene One

(IAN, ZANDER, and CHUCK's apartment. They lived there as college roommates and, two years into "real life" remain there. We are in the basement gameroom where they spend nearly 20 hours a day. There are no windows. There are 2 chairs and a couch facing the audience and every type of gaming equipment imaginable – rock band and guitar hero controllers, racing car steering wheel console, computers. We do not see the fourth wall of monitors, but we see their reflective glow.)

(As the audience filters in, ZANDER, IAN, CHUCK and JEANNIE are already playing, as they have been for hours. ZANDER has the steering wheel, playing a racing game. CHUCK plays guitar hero. JEANNIE is doing Dance Dance revolution. IAN is playing a World of Warcraft-type fantasy game on a computer keyboard. They each wear headphones, so they interact only with their individual screens, very intently. When the audience is in place, the lights fade.)

(Lights up on JEANNIE and CHUCK, seated on the couch with Xbox controllers in their hands. They are playing a Call of Duty-type war game and are deeply engaged in a military operation. CHUCK is intent on the game and delighted to be teaching the prettiest girl who has ever come to their basement. Their speech is high energy – they sometimes strain to be heard over the game, which we may or may not hear.)

JEANNIE. Because… I should live first.

CHUCK. Right?

JEANNIE. Get some real life experience. With actual kids.

7

CHUCK. Real life. Totally.

JEANNIE. But of course, my parents are like – what? I mean, everybody in my family went to med school – my siblings / and my…

CHUCK. Cool. Move around to the other side of the roof. I'm gonna shoot that guy. Please head shot, please head shot. YES!

JEANNIE. Ewwww. That was…

CHUCK. HA! Awesome, right?

JEANNIE. *(laughing)* Ok…

CHUCK. Try to stay behind me.

JEANNIE. Yeah.

    (They play for a beat.)

    So I'm taking the MCATS in case I want to be a psychiatrist eventually, but really, I'm like – why? To dole out pills? When what I really want is to interact with actual kids / you know?

CHUCK. Totally.

JEANNIE. In troubled neighborhoods. See what it's like in the trenches.

CHUCK. Right. Watch out here, we're surrounded.

JEANNIE. Not that there aren't plenty of troubled kids in regular schools, but if I go to some troubled neighborhoods, I think could really make a / difference.

CHUCK. Ya. Troubled neighborhoods – totally where you find the troubled kids.

JEANNIE. I mean, when you were in middle school, would / you have…

CHUCK. Let's go to that other rooftop.

JEANNIE. Oh. How do I…

CHUCK. You make him jump with this. See?

JEANNIE. Cool.

    (They go to the other rooftop.)

Would you have ever gone to your school psychologist with a real problem?

CHUCK. Nah.

JEANNIE. No way, right? And I so want to be that person, you know? Who / the kids feel..

CHUCK. Sure. Push this. To jump.

JEANNIE. …they can come to.

CHUCK. When they're troubled. Right.

JEANNIE. Does that sounds stupid? Like who the hell / am I that

CHUCK. No! Not at all. Jump! Now! Jump!

(He pushes the button on her controller.)

JEANNIE. Oh! Thanks.

CHUCK. Sure. No. It's totally awesome that you care. I mean so few people / really care.

JEANNIE. I do. I love kids. I really want to help.

(She shoots one of their own.)

CHUCK. Ahhh!

JEANNIE. Oh no! Sorry.

CHUCK. *(trying not to be upset)* No. It's cool.

JEANNIE. O.M.G. I just shot down one of / our own.

CHUCK. Happens all the time dude. Friendly fire. You're gonna lose some points though.

JEANNIE. *(She laughs.)* One of our own. I can't believe I'm even playing this!

CHUCK. You're doing great.

JEANNIE. Thanks. Did you apply to grad schools?/When you finished…

CHUCK. Nah.

Stay behind debris and stuff, ok? Did you see that sniper? You almost got shot.

JEANNIE. Oops. Sorry.

CHUCK. No. You're doing great.

JEANNIE. Thanks for killing him.

CHUCK. Call of duty baby.

JEANNIE. Hah!

CHUCK. I got your back.

(IAN enters, extremely agitated.)

IAN. Hey. Where's Zander?

JEANNIE. Hi Ian.

CHUCK. E-man! You were out! In the real world!

IAN. Have you seen him?
    Jeannie?!

JEANNIE. He was supposed to be here like…

IAN. *(texting ZAN)* Where is he?!

(They witness a crash.)

CHUCK AND JEANNIE. Nooooo!

IAN. I've been texting him for an hour.

(He exits to the back room.)

CHUCK. *(calling to IAN)* Hey. That guy came back again. He was asking some / crazy-ass things…

JEANNIE. Oh no! Chuck!

CHUCK. Ouch. Sorry dude.

JEANNIE. You hit me!

CHUCK. Shit. We need to find a tank and get out of here.

JEANNIE. But I'm… I'm dead now.

CHUCK. Look. You're fine. / See?

JEANNIE. What?

CHUCK. Pick yourself up. Dust yourself off…

JEANNIE. *(laughing)* Oh. Cool!

IAN. *(reentering)* When is he getting here?

CHUCK. *(laughing too)* Follow me.

IAN. Jeannie? Did you say?

JEANNIE. He was supposed to be here, like… *(the screen)* Yikes! …like hours ago. Why?

CHUCK. *(to JEANNIE)* Nice save.

JEANNIE. Thanks.

CHUCK. *(to* IAN*)* Dude, that suit came by again.

IAN. *(his phone)* God, Zan! Pick up!

JEANNIE. Who came by?

CHUCK. This creepy army dude is stalking Ian.

JEANNIE. What? Someone from / the army...

IAN. *(very important – to impress* JEANNIE*)* N.S.A.

CHUCK. He's come like three times. Only when Ian is out.
Which is like, never, so it's / totally...

JEANNIE. Wait. What?

CHUCK. They called his parents. His old professors. Uncle
Sam wants you dude. Bad.

JEANNIE. What do they want?

IAN. Now they want another interview. It's bogus.

JEANNIE. The army wants you? For a job?

IAN. NSA. Yup.

JEANNIE. O.M.G., what job?

IAN. If I tell you I'll have to kill you.

CHUCK. Are you gonna go? For the interview?

IAN. Nah.

CHUCK. Fuck, The National Security Agency? You should
go dude.

IAN. *(notices their game – forgets everything else)* Holy shit.
Is that Final Kill III?

CHUCK. Oh yeah, baby.

IAN. That's not out till next week!

CHUCK. Maybe for you.

IAN. How'd you get that? They broke the street date?

CHUCK. I have my ways.

IAN. Stellar graphics.

CHUCK. Right?

    (some catastrophe)

IAN. Ooooo. Epic fail. You guys suck.

JEANNIE. *(laughing)* We do / We really do.

CHUCK. Well, Jeannie sucks.

JEANNIE. Shut up. Why do you / need Zander?

CHUCK. Noooob. *(like "rube")* Bringing me down to your level.

IAN. He fucking sold my Exponent Potency Mask of the Algorith.

CHUCK. What?

IAN. On e-bay.

CHUCK. Holy shit.

JEANNIE. Your… Exponent…?

IAN. He auctioned it off.

CHUCK. No way.

JEANNIE. What's an / Ex….?

CHUCK. Exponent Potency Mask of the Algorith. It's this friggin' awesome, virtual… How much he get for it?

IAN. Last time I give that asshole my code.

JEANNIE. Z wouldn't do that – sell your…

IAN. I have the check. He fucking left me a check. He kept ten percent, and wrote me a check for the rest.

CHUCK. How much?

IAN. It's shit, man.

CHUCK. How much shit?

IAN. Nine.

(He kicks the table ineffectually.)

Dammit!

CHUCK. He got ten k for that thing?

JEANNIE. Wait. Ten thousand? Dollars?

CHUCK. Dude. That's awesome.

JEANNIE. Real American dollars? Ten thousand real American dollars?

CHUCK. I mean, isn't that awesome?

JEANNIE. For a make believe mask?

IAN. *(deeply insulted)* Make believe? That was a level thirty Exponent Potency Mask of the Algorith. That mask –

you put on that mask and you could do anything. Be anyone. Plus 53 Stamina. Plus 42 Agility. Increases your critical strike by ninety-fucking-seven. You know how many quests I won to level it up that high? You put on that mask, you enter the Jingpo Pakosphere, and you can defeat anyone.

(**ZANDER** *enters. He is all American, good looking.*)

ZANDER. All hail the conquering hero! I come bearing beer!

(*He goes to put it in the mini-frig.*)

IAN. Asshole!

ZANDER. Whoa. Ian. Did you see what I got you?

IAN. I saw what you left me.

ZANDER. Well, yeah, I took a percentage.

IAN. Stole.

ZANDER. Dude. It's a broker's fee. I mean, it's going to you for rent anyway, right?

JEANNIE. Hey, babe.

(**ZANDER** *goes over and kisses her.*)

ZANDER. Chuckstein. (*like "Einstein"*)

CHUCK. Hey.

IAN. You owe me twenty thousand dollars, Zander.

ZANDER. What?

CHUCK. Whoa.

IAN. That was a year's work there. That fucking mask is worth thirty k.

CHUCK. Holy shit.

JEANNIE. Wait. / What?

ZANDER. No Ian no. I asked around. I mean, I didn't sell to the first guy. I got offered 5k at first. I bargained it up. You should have seen / me. I…

IAN. I could have sold that mask for thirty thousand dollars. I would have lived off it…for like, FOREVER! And now – how the hell am I gonna see that money? *You're* never gonna get it! God!

CHUCK. Dude. Chill.

ZANDER. That mask was worth thirty? No way.

IAN. A guy in China just got 30k for a mask that didn't have half the powers of my mask.

ZANDER. Wow E, I'm totally sorry. You should have said something. I mean, I had no idea it was worth thirty. Wow. I mean / are you sure…

IAN. Said something? Said – "oh, by the way, please don't go sneaking into my account which I entrusted the code to you, and steal my mask?" Gee. It never occurred to me to tell you that. Next time I'll remember. / Thanks. Good advice.

ZANDER. You were going to get thirty for that mask? That's insane dude. That's totally/ insane.

IAN. What's insane is that you sold it for nothing. Dammit.

(He kicks the chair, ineffectually.)

CHUCK. Easy on the chair E. Innocent bystander.

JEANNIE. *(to ZANDER)* Call the guy back. The guy you sold it to. Tell him it was a mistake.

ZANDER. Babe.

JEANNIE. If you explain to him that it wasn't really your mask…maybe he'll understand.

IAN. And he'll just offer to pay an extra twenty grand.

JEANNIE. It's worth a try.

IAN. What planet do you live on?

CHUCK. Ian.

ZANDER. Oh God. I'm so sorry dude. Wow. Here, I thought I was gonna like…surprise you that I got this crazy dude / to pay…

IAN. Yeah. I'm surprised.

JEANNIE. Well, it's virtual, right? It's in a game? Can you make another one?

IAN. Make another one.

JEANNIE. I mean, you did it once, / right?

IAN. Do you know what it takes to get to that level? Only one other person in the WORLD has gotten to that level. And it was the guy in China. And he sold it for 30k. By the time I get there again, plenty of people will have gotten there and it's going to be worth shit. You're all so /…ignorant.

ZANDER. Hey. Come on.

IAN. You are. You're..

(It's pointless. Kicks the chair and hurts himself.)

Whatever. Ow. Forget it.

(He sits down in his chair and fires up the screen. Begins playing during this.)

CHUCK. He'll get you the money.

IAN. Right.

CHUCK. *(to* **ZANDER***)* Dude. You have to get him that money.

IAN. Forget it, Chuck.

JEANNIE. No. He will. Right, hon?

ZANDER. Yeah, wow. I mean, I had no idea it was worth that much. / Are you sure…

JEANNIE. But you have to. Pay him back.

ZANDER. Ok, I will.

IAN. Jeannie. He doesn't do anything. Don't you get that?

ZANDER. What is that supposed to mean?

JEANNIE. He does things.

IAN. Ummm…no.

JEANNIE. He'll get a job, right, babe? He'll pay you back a little at a time.

IAN. Uh huh.

JEANNIE. Right, babe?

CHUCK. Ou….ch. *(a bomb exploding at the end)*

ZANDER. Right.

IAN. What job? Ahhh! Forget it.

JEANNIE. He's had jobs. Right, Z?

CHUCK. Yeah, the thing is, with a job, you kind of have to show up.

IAN. He gets money off his parents. Don't you know that? All through school while I was here working...

ZANDER. Working?

IAN. His parents just sent him money.

ZANDER. Not any more!

IAN. Yeah, I noticed.

JEANNIE. *(to **ZANDER**)* Why don't you sell things too? Masks and...swords or whatnot. There must be other things worth a lot, I mean, you play tons...

CHUCK. Jeannie. Dude. Zan is totally not at that level.

ZANDER. Hey. Look. I'm plenty / respectable.

CHUCK. I mean, nothing personal dude, but that shit that Ian does, what he's capable of... that's like...it's like not even human. It's like not even in the same universe.

ZANDER. I've leveled up. Plenty. I was on level 37. On Quasar B. I had three level 70s with six more alts in the 30-45 range. But you know, I play a variety of games and /Ian just...

CHUCK. No way. Ian is like an artist. He's a total Nevcom genius.

JEANNIE. Yeah?

CHUCK. He was Nevada champion two years in a row. You didn't know that?

JEANNIE. Wow.

CHUCK. Nevada State Champion.

    *(to **ZANDER**)*

    You didn't tell her that dude?

ZANDER. Yeah / I did.

JEANNIE. Wow. No.

CHUCK. You are like, in the presence of greatness here.

IAN. *(flattered)* Shut up.

CHUCK. I'm serious dude. We are not worthy.

ZANDER. Well, excuse me if I'm not at his level, but, you know, I have a life. I don't play twenty hours a day.

CHUCK. You kinda do man.

ZANDER. I have a real life in the real world.

IAN. What? What is your real life? You can't even pay rent. I've been buying all the food.

ZANDER. I just bought beer!

IAN. What is your life? What do you do?

ZANDER. I have a girlfriend.

IAN. What does that mean? You're good at…what?

CHUCK. Getting a girlfriend!

JEANNIE. Ummm… I'm right here, so…

ZANDER. That's more than you dude. I mean, where's your girlfriend?

JEANNIE. Guys.

ZANDER. Have you ever had a girlfriend?

CHUCK. That's cold, Zan.

IAN. You're saying you're superior to me because you have a girlfriend.

ZANDER. No. I'm saying I have a LIFE because I have a girlfriend.

IAN. *(stymied)* What the fuck. Who has been CARRYING you?

ZANDER. What?

IAN. I have been fucking CARRYING you on my back since college.

ZANDER. That's bullshit.

IAN. Did you pay last month's rent?

ZANDER. I just left you a check.

IAN. YOU LEFT ME A CHECK OFF THE MONEY YOU STOLE FROM ME!

CHUCK. Owned!

IAN. You owe me last month's rent and next month's rent.

ZANDER. That's your real life. You're a slumlord.

IAN. Are you fucking out of your mind? I was stupid enough to put my name on the lease because I didn't expect you to welch out on me and then / steal my mask!

JEANNIE. Guys. Stop. Come on. You're best friends. Stop it.

ZANDER. Ian dude. I'm sorry about the mask. That was totally fucked of me and I'm sorry. I'll get you that money. I will. I'll...somehow I'll get it.

JEANNIE. Of course you will. Of course you'll pay him back. You're friends. That's what's really important.

CHUCK. Totally.

JEANNIE. This was a terrible mistake, but Zander will make it up to you. You guys should just like, go out for a beer or something, you know? Or a movie? Get outside and hang out, right?

CHUCK. Outside?

IAN. I'm meeting a bunch of guys on Paraquad. But thanks.

JEANNIE. Online?

(IAN fires up his game. CHUCK and ZANDER are mesmerized watching him play.)

Let's all get out in the fresh air. Go for a walk or something. We'll all feel better.

(Pause. They don't even hear her.)

I was reading in my Psych 3 about internet addiction, which I'm *not* saying you have – at *all,* I'm just saying they think it's associated with reduced levels of dopaminergic receptor availability in the striatum. Which basically means, it can make you like totally depressed.

CHUCK. Huh. That's really interesting.

JEANNIE. Dopamine is a powerful drug.

ZANDER. That's fascinating, babe. Maybe you're depressed E-man.

IAN. *(playing intently)* I'm depressed you fucking gave away my fucking mask for fucking nothing!

ZANDER. Yeah, but listen – Jeannie's right. You do take this whole gaming thing too seriously man.

IAN. What?

ZANDER. You need more dopamine. You're all uptight because you have nothing real in your life. You need to get off the screen. For your own good. You need to get a life man.

IAN. I have – ALL OF THIS

(pointing to all the equipment)

I bought – ALL OF THIS. With gaming money, with tournament money, with money I EARN. Leveling up other people, selling swords, turbo clubs…

ZANDER. Out of this box, I mean. You have nothing /out of this…

IAN. And you play it. You play all of it as much as I do. You play all day and all night and you don't sleep and you forget to go to work and you stand up your girlfriend and all your "real life" things that are so fantastic, because you play as much as I do. More. But you are BAD at it. If I put in as many hours as you do at something, and I was still bad at it, I'd freaking kill myself.

(There is a silence. Everyone is shocked by the force of that statement.)

ZANDER. Wow.

JEANNIE. He's just upset, honey. We / should all…

ZANDER. No. I'm done. That's fine. That's cool. I'm done. I'm not playing any more.

CHUCK. Dude. Don't even say that.

ZANDER. I don't need to play your shit.

IAN. Good. Go get some dopamine.

CHUCK. What will you play, dude? I mean, I have the Wii. You're always welcome to…

ZANDER. And I don't need to live here.

IAN. Whatever.

CHUCK. Yo. Cool out. This is totally extreme.

ZANDER. I'll get my own place.

IAN. Great.

CHUCK. Come on.

ZANDER. *(to* JEANNIE*)* Or I can move in with you. Wouldn't that be awesome? If we…

JEANNIE. Well…my roommates would kind / of freak if…

CHUCK. Hey. Come on. Let's just chill. How about some Ramen noodles? *(pause)* Guys? I'll cook.

ZANDER. Look. I'll find a way to pay you back.

IAN. Yeah.

ZANDER. No. I will. I'm sorry. I didn't think… I didn't know it was worth that much.

IAN. It was the whole breaking into my system and…

ZANDER. No. No, I know. I'll never… That was fucked up. I'm sorry.

IAN. Ok.

ZANDER. Yeah? We're cool?

(pause)

IAN. I have a life.

ZANDER. Ok.

IAN. I do. I have…people…in my life. *(referring to the screen)* Those people are…

ZANDER. Well…

IAN. What?

ZANDER. They're not real. This is what we're saying.

IAN. They're not real people. Playing. On their systems. Just like I am. Those are not real people.

ZANDER. The gamers are real but you don't actually know them. I mean, dude, you don't actually ever leave this room.

IAN. I do so.

ZANDER. Well…not really. I mean, barely.

(There is a beat as they all process that.)

IAN. *(referring to outside)* What makes that so much better?

CHUCK. Uh…reality dude.

IAN. No really, why should I do that instead of this?

JEANNIE. Ian, you can't spend your whole life playing games.

IAN. I am making a living. A real living. Most people spend fifty hours a week at some job they freakin' hate and go home to people they find boring and it's the same fucking thing day after day…

JEANNIE. But it doesn't have to be that. Real life can have meaning, Ian. Striving for some goal, that will bring, you know…satisfaction, and, and joy, and…

IAN. Where's the epic win in life? There's no epic win. Ever.

JEANNIE. Epic win?

IAN. Where's the noble quest that requires a band of really smart, capable people.

CHUCK. Or Klarnogs, or Santorgs.

IAN. Those people I work with – those people – I can choose who I am, who I want to be – I can be myself with those people.

CHUCK. Or a Klarnog. Or a Santorg.

IAN. They don't care what I look like here. They don't want to make idiotic small talk about things I don't care about or know about – all that superficial crap. It's not about that there. They show up and they work at optimum capacity so we can all achieve our goals.

Fucking awesome talented, smart – Those are my people. That's who I spend my time with.

You may think it's less real because they're not here in this room, but that just shows your limitations, not mine. Those people I play with – none of them would ever use my code and break in and…

ZANDER. Fuck! I said I was sorry! And you don't know that. You don't know a fucking thing about those people.

IAN. I know them better than I know you.

JEANNIE. Wow.

CHUCK. E.

    (pause)

JEANNIE. Ian, finding someone to love is like that epic win, you know? Thrilling, surprising things can happen, Ian. Really. Any day something amazing might happen if you just go out and look for it. That day Zan asked me out...

ZANDER. Aww, babe.

    (He kisses her.)

    (CHUCK *makes a gagging noise.)*

JEANNIE. You need to go out and find someone who makes you feel like life is worth living.

    (Pause. **IAN** *is struck hard by this.)*

ZANDER. Dude. Ian. I'm sorry, man. I am.

IAN. Uh huh.

ZANDER. And I will. Pay you back. Get a...job. I will. A real job.

IAN. Ya. Me too. I can get a real job.

CHUCK. What?

IAN. I'm going to get a real job. In the real world. Faster than you.

ZANDER. You are?

IAN. Yeah. I'm going to fucking get that job with the N.S.A.

Scene Two

*(JEANNIE and CHUCK have begun a role-playing game.
He has her keyboard, creating her character.)*

JEANNIE. Don't you see awful things? People losing everything...

CHUCK. It's pretty intense. *(the screen)* There.

JEANNIE. That haircut is so cute! I love it.

CHUCK. Good. Now we have to dress you.

JEANNIE. I'm dressed.

CHUCK. That's standard issue. We'll find something that's more "you".

JEANNIE. Oh! Fun!
So why did you choose black jack? Or do they /choose for you?

CHUCK. I used to deal Roulette, but I hated it. It was all luck. And these guys come in, they think they've got a strategy, I'm like, dude – wake up. There is no strategy. That was sad.
Here, I'll give you some credits.

JEANNIE. What's that? Can't I earn them?

CHUCK. Don't worry. You'll pay me back. Mwah hah hah.

JEANNIE. Yikes.

CHUCK. Ok. You have 200.

JEANNIE. Wow. That's a lot. Are you sure...

CHUCK. *(laughing)* You don't even know what they are!

JEANNIE. Ok ok.

CHUCK. Here. Let me take you to the store.

JEANNIE. So isn't black jack just luck?

CHUCK. Yeah, but there's skill too. And these guys, card counters, try to beat the system, and every once in a while they do. I like that. It's a real game, you know? If you can't win, it's not a real game.

JEANNIE. But working all night. Don't you lose track of...

CHUCK. Yeah. Totally. No windows. No clocks. The drinks are flowing. It's the twilight zone.

JEANNIE. *(the basement)* It's like down here.

CHUCK. Hah! Right!

JEANNIE. *(the game)* OK. So now what do I do?

CHUCK. Let's shop. Here. Stop me when you see a top you like.

JEANNIE. Ok. So, is there something else you want to do? Like a career or… I mean, do you have plans?

CHUCK. Nope. Stop me when you see one.

JEANNIE. No. Eww. No. No. Stop! That's cute!

CHUCK. What?

JEANNIE. Why not?

CHUCK. Too frumpy.

JEANNIE. It's a peasant blouse.

CHUCK. Let's keep looking.

JEANNIE. Fine. No. No.

CHUCK. Ahhhh! Yes!

JEANNIE. Chuck!

CHUCK. What?

JEANNIE. I'm not gonna wear that!

CHUCK. Jeannie. This is a chance to expand your comfort zone. Risk free. What color do you like?

JEANNIE. Blue.

CHUCK. Which blue? Here, let me show you.

JEANNIE. This is so goofy. I don't even like shopping in life.

CHUCK. What kind of chick are you?

JEANNIE. Shut up. That's good. I like that one.

CHUCK. Peacock, eh? Awesome. You're going to look hot in that.

JEANNIE. Maybe my character isn't hot.

CHUCK. I have a feeling she's way hot. Skirt or jeans. Or shorts?

JEANNIE. What do you like?

CHUCK. Up to you.

JEANNIE. Oh, now it's up to me?

CHUCK. It's always up to you. I'm just the facilitator.

JEANNIE. Skirt.

CHUCK. Excellent choice.

JEANNIE. That one. That's cute.

CHUCK. Jeannie.

JEANNIE. Yeah?

CHUCK. My grandmother has a skirt like that.

JEANNIE. This is what… Daphne likes.

CHUCK. Ahhh.. Daphne. Hot name.

JEANNIE. Who are you?

CHUCK. I'm Earl.

JEANNIE. HAH! Earl!?

CHUCK. Earl thinks Daphne would wear…this skirt.

JEANNIE. Daphne would not leave the house in that skirt.

CHUCK. Maybe she's staying in today.

JEANNIE. Chuck.

CHUCK. It's totally hot.

Earl thinks Daphne would wear these shoes.

JEANNIE. *(laughing)* Earl's either a secret cross-dresser or a pimp.

CHUCK. Earl respects Daphne and wants her to feel good about herself. In whatever clothes he chooses. Here's a cute little handbag.

JEANNIE. Oh my God.

CHUCK. Wow. You look awesome.

JEANNIE. Don't let Daphne's mom see her in that outfit.

CHUCK. Daphne's mom lives like four hundred miles away. In… Fresno.

JEANNIE. Daphne did not grow up in Fresno!

CHUCK. Daphne is new in town. And Earl is going to show her around.

(**CHUCK** *hands the keyboard back to* **JEANNIE** *and picks up his own.*)

Come to Earl's pad, Daphne.

JEANNIE. I don't think I should.

CHUCK. You definitely should.

JEANNIE. Well, only for a few minutes. I need to study before my Adolescent Psychology class.

CHUCK. Blow it off.

JEANNIE. Noooo. Hey. Nice place, Earl.

CHUCK. Thanks. Have a seat. On the couch. I'll get you something to drink.

JEANNIE. I like your artwork.

CHUCK. Cost a fortune. Earl has expensive taste.

JEANNIE. Not in girls.

CHUCK. Hah. Here you go.

JEANNIE. *(laughing)* Martinis? Who are you?

CHUCK. Cheers.

(He types something.)

JEANNIE. Why type – it's just easier to talk.

CHUCK. But that's Earl talking.

(JEANNIE laughs, and then types. He types something back. It is very suggestive. She looks at him, surprised.)

JEANNIE. Chuck!

CHUCK. Earl. Type it.

(She does. He types back. She types back something that surprises him. She is starting to play along. He looks at her. She looks at him, then back at the screen. Types again. He's amazed. And excited. He types back quickly. Then she does. They are both getting very aroused. He types.)

JEANNIE. No.

CHUCK. No?

JEANNIE. That's…we shouldn't.

CHUCK. We're not. They are.

(She types something. He laughs and types back. She pauses. Considers this. Types again.)

Mmmmm. Wow. Babe.

JEANNIE. Type it.

(He does. They have moved a bit closer on the couch, but are very tense about what is happening between them. They are breathing heavily. Typing fast and furious, over each other. More and more intense.)

How do I make her move?

(He shows her on her controller.)

How do I move her leg?

(He shows her.)

How do I move her hand?

(He shows her. She moves her character.)

CHUCK. Oh my God.

(They stop typing and just move their characters and watch, transfixed. They each occasionally involuntarily moan. This goes on for several moments.)

(ZANDER bursts in with a large box.. They quickly fumble with their controllers in a panic, turn off the screen. JEANNIE jumps up quickly, guiltily.)

ZANDER. I have had the most fan-fucking-tastic day!

(He grabs JEANNIE and gives her a long kiss, which is awkward for her and for CHUCK.)

Man! Anybody want a beer?

(He goes to the fridge.)

CHUCK. Sure dude. Thanks.

ZANDER. Hey, babe, you want?

JEANNIE. *(still flustered)* Hey! No. Thanks. I should go… study.

ZANDER. Blow it off. You don't need to study any more. You're going to be a millionaire.

JEANNIE. What happened?

CHUCK. Did a rich uncle die?

ZANDER. *(bringing over the beers)* I went to this seminar today. What is today? Mark this day on the calendar! I went to this seminar that is going to fucking change our lives.

JEANNIE. Wow.

CHUCK. Is this a cult, Z? Do we need to deprogram you? Exorcism?

ZANDER. Joke on funny boy. This is easy easy money.

CHUCK. Ruh roh.

ZANDER. Where's Ian?

CHUCK. Off peeing in a cup.

ZANDER. Shit. I want him to hear this too. Oh well.

(going through the box) It's called – Proneutra. It's this awesome supplement…but that's just the… the physical product. The thing you can hold. What it really is, it's a way of life.

JEANNIE. Yeah? I thought you had a job interview.

ZANDER. Baby, this is so much bigger than that. I'm not going to work for anyone else ever again.

CHUCK. Again? When / did you ever…

ZANDER. I'm the head of my own company now. And I can bring in everybody. I want all the people I care about to get in on this while it's in its early stages. The ground floor. Because, over time, all it does is grow.

CHUCK. Like this?

(He makes a pyramid with his hands.)

ZANDER. Listen. It's like capital. Eventually, it just grows by itself, while you're not even looking. You find other people, other…entrepreneurs, who want to own something, be part of something big, like yourselves…

*(**CHUCK** looks behind him.)*

And you get them in on it. And then they get their friends on board…

CHUCK. It's a pyramid scheme.

ZANDER. God Chuck! I knew you would say that. No! It's NOT. Ok, it is, but so what – it's a fucking awesome product. It's…

(He grabs a brochure and consults it.)

…multi-level marketing. Here – look at the literature. Don't go judging it, bringing all this negativity to it, until you read it. And try the stuff. They gave me one supplement, early in the day. And look at me.

JEANNIE. Yeah?

ZANDER. Don't I look different to you?

JEANNIE. Maybe…

ZANDER. I feel totally different. I feel powerful, babe. I feel like I could take on the world. And they have supplements for everything. I mean, you gear it to the client's specific needs. Does he want to boost energy, endurance, brain function, metabolism, *(glancing at the brochure)* anaerobic threshold – see? It's scientific man. It's totally… You have to read the materials.

(He's back to rifling through the box he brought in.)

JEANNIE. So…it's vitamins. Right? Are you selling…?

ZANDER. But it's not. Or it is, but it's way more than that. Once I get some more training – they have these periodic…

*(**IAN** enters during this. He is wearing a short sleeve button-down shirt and a tie, which he takes off.)*

CHUCK. E-man. Dude. How'd it go?

*(**IAN** sits right down at his computer and starts playing.)*

IAN. Hey guys.

CHUCK. Did you get the job? What is the job?

IAN. They're still trying to establish whether I'm a psychopath. And whether my blood and urine are government quality.

CHUCK. And what's the verdict? Psychopath or just sociopath?

JEANNIE. Did they tell you? What the job is?

IAN. They were commendably vague. Chaney vague.

CHUCK. How did they find you? I mean, why you?

IAN. My mad gaming skills and Ninja reflexes.

ZANDER. Dude. Fuck working for the government. I've got this opportunity for you. For all of us.

IAN. Yeah?

CHUCK. Zan's joined a cult.

ZANDER. Shut the fuck up.

(He goes to the box and pulls out a few bottles of pills.)

Here. Ian. Take this. You'll feel fantastic.

IAN. Drug dealer? This is the opportunity?

ZANDER. Just take one.

IAN. Is the first one free?

CHUCK. *(laughing)* Fail, Z!

ZANDER. Just try it.

CHUCK. Epic fail.

IAN. Dude. I'm going to be peeing in cups for the next year. No thanks.

ZANDER. It's good for you man.

IAN. Is this nine to five drug dealing? What are they paying you?

ZANDER. It's not that kind of job.

IAN. The kind where they pay you?

ZANDER. Stop for a minute and look at the literature.

(He holds out the brochures which IAN *ignores, as he's still madly playing.)*

Come on. These supplements are cutting-edge…

IAN. Dude. Vitamins are an illusion. They don't do anything. It's proven. All they give you is expensive pee.

CHUCK. Man, you are totally obsessed with pee now.

IAN. Where are you going to peddle your wares? Besides this apartment?

ZANDER. Well, I only have samples now. But once I get five more people to sell, they'll give me the product.

JEANNIE. You have to get other people to sell in order to sell?

ZANDER. Well, with you three on-board, I only need two more.

JEANNIE. And then we would have to get five more people to sell? Each?

IAN. You're catching on.

JEANNIE. I don't know, babe.

CHUCK. I totally know. I'm out. But, umm…thanks for thinking of me.

IAN. Dude! It's a scam!

ZANDER. You're so closed minded. This is going to be one of those things where, ten years from now when I'm on my yacht and sending you postcards from Barbados or wherever, you're going to be thinking – damn, I could have been in on that at the beginning, but I was a total asshole.

CHUCK. You'd send me a postcard, Z?

ZANDER. I'm serious guys. It's your loss.

JEANNIE. So…is that all? You have to get five people and then you get the product?

ZANDER. Just about. Hey, when's your next class, babe?

JEANNIE. I've got Adolescent Psych at 5. I should really be studying.

ZANDER. Maybe I'll tag along – if we go a little early I can talk to some of the kids. See if I can drum up some interest.

JEANNIE. Ok. I guess. I don't know if Professor Maxwell / would like…

ZANDER. Outside the class. I'm not an idiot. I'll just hang out with you outside the class before-hand. Cool?

JEANNIE. Ok. I guess.

ZANDER. Dana would be good at selling I think.

JEANNIE. Why Dana?

ZANDER. She looks kind of healthy and athletic. I'd buy vitamins off her.

JEANNIE. Dana?

CHUCK. Oh snap.

JEANNIE. I don't think she's ever worked out a day in her life.

ZANDER. Yeah? She's got that kind of athletic...

JEANNIE. I don't even think she owns sneakers.

ZANDER. Well, whoever you think, babe. You know them better than I do. But I'm raring to go! Should we head over?

JEANNIE. It's a little early. I should really study first.

ZANDER. We can hang at the library. While you study I can drum up some future...

CHUCK. Entrepreneurs. Like ourselves.

JEANNIE. Ok.

(He grabs her and gives her a long kiss.)

Ok. I'll get my books together.

(She goes upstairs.)

ZANDER. Cool. I'll be right up.

So Ian, I need you to do me a solid.

IAN. Zan. Give up. I'm not pushing your product.

ZANDER. Nooo. That's fucked up, but that's not it. See, there are some minor start-up fees/ just for the first...

CHUCK. Oh shit! Dude!

ZANDER. No. Just to get started. I have to give them five hundred.

IAN. You have to pay them to sell their vitamins.

ZANDER. You just have to put money down to – these vitamins are not like what you get at CVS, dude. This is some highly developed, scientifically...developed shit. They can't just let you walk out the door with this valuable shit without something down.

IAN. No, dude. No.

ZANDER. I'm not asking for a handout, E. I'm just saying, could you hold off cashing that check?

JEANNIE. *(from offstage)* You coming, hon?

ZANDER. Ya. Right there, baby!

Thanks a million, E. You'll see that money with interest, within a week. I'm sure of it.

(He runs upstairs. CHUCK *and* IAN *look at each other and crack up.)*

CHUCK. Few rounds of Final Kill?

(He sits down and fires up the program.)

IAN. Sure. What the fuck.

(They fire it up and begin maniacally pressing their controllers, transfixed on the screen. We hear the sounds of bombs, machine guns, screams, soldiers shouting.)

CHUCK. Is that an / RPG?

IAN. Dude, it's an RPG! Fire!

CHUCK. Ahhhhhhh!

Scene Three

(Lights up on ZANDER, JEANNIE *and* CHUCK *all playing very intently together. Probably a fantasy role-playing game.)*

JEANNIE. OMG. What is that thing?! Where did it come from?

CHUCK. Santorg. That club has death rays, so use your shield.

JEANNIE. Yikes.

CHUCK. He's a shape shifter. We've seen him before.

JEANNIE. A shape shifter?

ZANDER. Let's climb the back of that cliff. Come on, babe.

CHUCK. Remember that chick with the same club? That was him.

JEANNIE. Why would he look like that when he could look like her?

(IAN comes bursting in, in high spirits.)

IAN. Huzzah! Good day, good peoples!

CHUCK. E-man! Grab a controller. We're about to battle a Santorg

JEANNIE. We are?

IAN. Cool.

(He grabs a controller and joins them.)

Why are we up this cliff?

JEANNIE. Wait. What time is it? Oh shit! I missed my Early Childhood Development class. Shit shit shit!

ZANDER. Babe, you're a senior. It doesn't matter any more.

JEANNIE. It does if I want to go to grad school. Oh shit.

ZANDER. You've got like a 3.9. Relax.

JEANNIE. We've been playing for four hours?

IAN. Stand back, guys.

(He clearly brings out the heavy artillery. We hear roaring and then moaning from the Santorg as **IAN** *slays him. They are done with this level and stop playing.)*

CHUCK. Awesome, dude.

JEANNIE. That was amazing. What was that thing – like a lazar? Where did you get that?

CHUCK. Ian's leveled to 49. He's got all the fun toys.

ZANDER. He really shouldn't be on our quest. It's not right.

CHUCK. Why not?

ZANDER. He should be on his own quest. For his level.

CHUCK. That's bogus.

ZANDER. You should fight at your own level.

IAN. *(He goes to his screen.)* It's cool. I need to clock in on Paraquad. Some dude in New York is paying me a buttload to get him achievements.

JEANNIE. What does that mean?

IAN. I sign in and level him up so he can play his little Wall Street friends and kick their butts.

JEANNIE. You can play for someone else?

ZANDER. It's wrong. It totally taints the games.

CHUCK. Like you don't buy cheats.

ZANDER. I don't man.

CHUCK. Right.

ZANDER. I don't. I wouldn't do that.

CHUCK. Ok.

ZANDER. I don't, Chuck!

CHUCK. Ok, Dude!

JEANNIE. So, people pay you to play?

IAN. To level them up.

JEANNIE. Really?

IAN. There are warehouses in China with kids playing all day and night to level up these crazy rich guys for like two hundred a week. I can make twice that easy.

JEANNIE. Wow.

CHUCK. And how was your day at the office, dear?

IAN. It was totally outrageously awesome. I passed the wacko test, and now I'm officially employed. They're training me.

ZANDER. Doing what? Just tell us something dude. Training you to what?

IAN. Can't say. But I said on the polygraph that I haven't smoked pot in two years, and I passed. So…if someone calls…

CHUCK. Ha! Me too. No pot. No beer.

(He downs his beer.)

JEANNIE. My dad said they're training gamers to do remote missile launches of… / what is it?

IAN. Why did your dad say that?

JEANNIE. Oh, I told him about how you were interviewing with the NSA / and he said that maybe…

IAN. You told him? Why would you tell him that? Shit. Why would you say that? To your dad?

JEANNIE. I'm sorry. I / didn't think that…

CHUCK. Chill dude.

IAN. What exactly did you tell him?

JEANNIE. I just said that you had an interview. I mean, that you were this amazing player. Gamer. And that you had this interview with the NSA. That's all. That's all I know. So…

IAN. And he said…

JEANNIE. And he said that maybe they were recruiting you. To do, you know, these remote missile things. Drones! That you were probably operating these drones.

CHUCK. Holy shit. Is that what you're doing, E?

ZANDER. Probably doing some desk job, and he's just trying to make it seem like he's hot / shit.

IAN. I'm not doing anything yet. I'm just in training. And don't say anything to anybody. Any of you. I mean it. I signed a stack of papers. That I'm not going to tell anyone, not even my family, what I'm doing. What they want me to do.

ZANDER. Yeah, you also said you haven't smoked pot.

IAN. Look. I want this thing. I want this job. You said I didn't have a real life, right? I should get a life. So now I have a real life, ok? A real job. That I go to every day. So just don't say anything more to anybody.

JEANNIE. I won't. I'm really sorry Ian. / I won't.

ZANDER. She fucking said she wouldn't asshole. You have to be so self important about this whole thing. It's so top secret. You signed a / fucking paper.

CHUCK. Wow, Ian. That's so cool. I mean, if that's what you're doing.

IAN. Yeah. It's pretty mind blowing. If that's what I'm doing.

CHUCK. They use you, I mean, these guys they hire, they use them even if they aren't military?

IAN. Well, I'm not the pilot. I'm the S.O. – sensor operator. These awesome pilots who've had years and years in real combat, you know, on the actual field of play, they fly the plane, fire the missiles.

CHUCK. That is so unreal…

IAN. And then the sensor operators use these laser instruments to make sure it goes to its target. And aim these awesome million dollar cameras that can see fucking everything. So, of course they need people with top-notch skills, you know? Gamers, the top gamers, have awesome reflexes.

JEANNIE. My dad said…oh. Never mind. Sorry.

CHUCK. No, what? We're not talking about you, Ian, we're just talking about these guys, not you. I mean, if Jeannie's dad knows about it and he's a…

JEANNIE. Dentist.

CHUCK. He's a fucking dentist, then it can't be that top secret. Right?

IAN. How does your dad know all this?

JEANNIE. He like, read it in the paper. Sorry.

ZANDER. *(howling)* HAH! He read it in the fucking paper! Pwnd *("poned")* Ian. It's so top secret! It's in the friggin' news.

IAN. Did I say it was top secret?

ZANDER. What else did your dad read, babe? In the fucking Reno Gazette Journal?

(JEANNIE *looks anxiously to* IAN.)

IAN. It's cool. I mean, you can talk about what your dad read. It's got nothing to do with me.

JEANNIE. Well, he said most of the missile, or drone attacks in…

IAN. The Preditor. And the Reaper is the new one.

CHUCK. Wow.

JEANNIE. in Afghanistan and Iraq…

IAN. UAVs. Unmanned Aerial Vehicles.

JEANNIE. Yeah. They're operated out of here, out of Nevada.

IAN. Creech

CHUCK. Cool.

IAN. Airforce Base.

JEANNIE. And that they use kids, gamers 'cause there's no way to train people as much as… I mean, no matter how much some pilot could train, he wouldn't have been putting in 20 hours a day for years and years.

IAN. Plus, they're running out of pilots. There are more unmanned vehicles than manned planes. It's insane. They need more people fast. They'll give me like thirty hours of flight training and then…

CHUCK. Holy shit!

ZANDER. How many guys do they need? Are they looking for more gamers?

CHUCK. *(laughing)* Z! You were just ragging on this whole situation. What about your business, dude? You're your own boss, remember?

ZANDER. Hey, I totally don't need to work for the government. Clock in clock out. How many hours you work?

IAN. It's going to be fourteen hour days for a while.

CHUCK. Holy shit.

ZANDER. Fuck that! All I need is two more recruits and I get the product. Maybe Karen, right, babe?

JEANNIE. I dunno.

CHUCK. But Ian, this thing is nuts. I mean, you have your hand on the button? What if you fuck up?

IAN. It's not like that. It takes like seventeen steps to fire anything. It would be pretty / hard to…

CHUCK. Holy shit. It's so outrageously cool. You're like a spy.

IAN. Did your dad read about this? For surveillance, they also have these cameras in like, little hand operated planes. Like remote control toys. Your dad read about this, right? I mean, this is general knowledge.

JEANNIE. I guess.

CHUCK. Sure he did.

IAN. And on the screen, it's so mind-blowingly cool – it's like you can see everything. It's as good as any shooter game. Better.

CHUCK. Amazing. You are like, the luckiest dude in America.

ZANDER. What's the big deal? If it's just like the games. He's doing the same thing we're doing, but he has to drive fifty miles to do it.

CHUCK. It's REAL.

How long do you train? When do you start really bombing shit?

IAN. They don't tell you. You have to be totally perfect for a long time, and then – boom – sometimes you're doing practice missions, sometimes you're doing real ones. You don't know. So it doesn't fuck with your mind when you blow out a village, you know? You might have done it, or it might have just been another simulation.

JEANNIE. But, you're going to really be killing real people.

IAN. Or not.

JEANNIE. But eventually you will. I mean, it stands to reason that you eventually will. If you keep at it.

IAN. Oh, I'm keeping at it.

JEANNIE. And then... I mean, doesn't that bother you?

IAN. Dude, did you hear what I said? I won't know. I won't know when it's real. Look, it's not as if I'm doing it. I don't give the orders. I don't even know who gives the orders. By the time it gets down to me, it's passed through ten guys. Sometimes I'm just, I mean sometimes the S.O. is just surveilling the area. I'm like, the defense. Sometimes.

JEANNIE. I guess.

IAN. And if they didn't use me, they would use somebody else. They're going to do it. With or without me. But if they use me, they know it'll be done right. Innocent people won't get killed. Because I'm incredibly skilled. I'll get my target. I won't fuck up. So really, I'm probably saving lives doing it. I'll make sure it's done right.

JEANNIE. No, you're right. It's good that it's someone who's really amazing and accurate. You're totally right. I just mean I couldn't do it.

ZANDER. Yeah. I couldn't knowingly kill people.

CHUCK. Hah! You were just drooling over it dude.

ZANDER. And you know that there are always innocent casualties in these things. No matter how accurate you are. I mean, it even happens in the games.

IAN. Well, yeah, sometimes mistakes get made. That's part of war.

ZANDER. Then why do it? If you're / killing innocent...

IAN. So you're saying there should never be any military action. What about fucking World War II? Are you saying we should have stayed out of WWII?

ZANDER. No.

IAN. So there should be killing, you just shouldn't have to do it. Let somebody else do it. Let somebody else have blood on his hands.

ZANDER. You don't have blood on your hands. You have a little controller in your hands. The blood is like thousands of miles away. You're in some air / conditioned...

CHUCK. Dude. Let's just... It's a totally cool job. I'm jealous as shit. You are going to learn things and see things... we can't even dream of.

IAN. Thanks, man.

(He sits down at his screen and fires up. CHUCK *goes to his screen.)*

JEANNIE. I can't believe I missed my class. Damn. And I like that class.

ZANDER. So let's go over there. You can get the notes from one of the other kids, right? And I need to talk to Karen. She's so close to signing on.

JEANNIE. I'd hate to run into Casey. She's such an awesome professor. And why did I miss her class? What excuse do I give? Video games? / Damn.

ZANDER. Hah! You are so fucking sweet, babe. They don't notice who's there.

JEANNIE. I dunno.

ZANDER. Come on. I'll walk you over.

JEANNIE. I don't know where Karen's going to come up with 500 dollars, Z. I don't think...

(He gives her a kiss.)

ZANDER. Don't worry. They all say they can't find the money, and then they do. Laterz.

CHUCK. Bye, Z. Jeannie.

JEANNIE. Bye, guys.

(They leave.)

IAN. You know, if you want to come interview, I could get you in.

CHUCK. What? Really?

IAN. I mean, no promise they'll sign you on, but they did say if I know anybody with serious skills…

CHUCK. Wow. Thanks. That's so awesome dude.

IAN. No problem.

CHUCK. I really appreciate that.

IAN. I'll give'm your name.

CHUCK. Yeah. But…you know, I don't think so.

IAN. Why not? Come on. You meet with them. They give you a bunch of tests.

CHUCK. I've kind of got things good at the casino.

IAN. Dude, how long can you stay there? That's a bad scene. You're gonna burn out, man.

CHUCK. Maybe.

IAN. Come on. You're a smart guy.

CHUCK. Nah.

IAN. You need a fucking career. You / can't just…

CHUCK. I don't know. Maybe I'll go back to grad school. You know, in a few years. I don't know.

IAN. Well, think about it.

CHUCK. Ok. I appreciate the offer, E. I really do. Thanks.

IAN. It's cool.

(They each put on headsets and start madly playing in their own private games.)

Scene Four

(IAN is at his screen. We hear JEANNIE come in upstairs.)

JEANNIE. Zan?

(IAN has his headphones on and doesn't hear. She comes down the stairs and sees him playing.)

Hey, Ian, have you seen Zander?

(He doesn't hear her. She stands behind him and watches him play for a moment. Touches his shoulder.)

IAN. *(jumps)* Shit! Don't sneak up on me.

(He takes off his headset, but goes back to playing.)

JEANNIE. Sorry. Do you know where / Zan is?

IAN. Nope.

JEANNIE. We were supposed to meet at the student union two hours ago. He's not answering my texts.

IAN. How strange.

JEANNIE. I'm sure he just got caught up in his recruiting. He's really into it.

(pause)

I should be studying anyway. Finals are in three weeks.

JEANNIE. *(Nothing from IAN. He just continues playing.)* It's totally freaking me out. That this is it, you know?

(nothing from IAN)

Did you feel that way? Your last semester?

IAN. No.

JEANNIE. Did you apply to grad school and stuff? Oh – duh. Obviously not. I'm kind of glad I didn't and I'm also a little freaked, you know? At least with grad school, you have a few years to put off real life, right?

IAN. Hm.

JEANNIE. But… I figured, no – time to grow up. Actually spend some time working with kids. Get to know them, rather than read about them in a text book.

IAN. That should do it.

(No idea what this means. She watches him play for a bit.)

JEANNIE. Wow. You're flying. It's beautiful. You're so good at this.

(As she watches him fly, he looks at her. She's so beautiful.)

It's like watching an amazing athlete like...

Oh my God, I can't think of any athletes! What is wrong with me? All I can think of is that kid who smoked pot – the swimmer? Michael...

(He is caught staring and goes back to his game. She watches him for a while.)

Do you mind me watching you?

IAN. No.

JEANNIE. It's not distracting?

IAN. If you stopped talking I would probably forget you're here.

JEANNIE. Oh. Ok.

(She sits beside him.)

Do you want me to stop talking?

(He doesn't say anything.)

You don't like me, do you.

IAN. I have no real feeling either way.

JEANNIE. Why?

IAN. ...I don't understand what you're asking.

JEANNIE. Is it because I'm Zan's girlfriend and the two of you are best friends and you feel that I'm kind of usurping your place, or...taking up the time you would usually spend together?

IAN. You've been studying that psych.

JEANNIE. You think I'm a total idiot, don't you?

IAN. *(making a joke)* Well...total?

(She gets up.)

JEANNIE. Fine.

IAN. Why are you with him?

JEANNIE. What? Zander?

IAN. No. Michael Jordan.

JEANNIE. Huh?

IAN. That's the name of a remarkable athlete, by the way. Next time you're trying to come up with a sports simile.

JEANNIE. You want to know why I like Zander?

(IAN sighs.)

I like him cause he's smart and funny and…

IAN. Is he smart? Or funny?

JEANNIE. You don't think so?

(no answer)

Sorry. I think he is.

IAN. Ok.

JEANNIE. Well, he's like, your best friend. Why do you like him?

IAN. Do I like him?

JEANNIE. You've lived together for five years…

IAN. Right.

JEANNIE. And Chuck too, right? For like four years?

IAN. You've done your girlfriend due diligence.

JEANNIE. So why do you live with them?

IAN. Chuck's a great guy actually. And I can't afford the whole place myself.

JEANNIE. Then find other people you want to live with.

IAN. Who?

JEANNIE. There's nobody you like.

IAN. I enjoy many of the people I game with.

JEANNIE. Ian, you really don't know those people.

IAN. But I guess you really know Zan.

(pause)

JEANNIE. Zan considers you his best friend.

IAN. Sad.

JEANNIE. It's sad for you.

IAN. Why is that?

JEANNIE. Because Zan really likes you. He's getting something out of the relationship. And, you're not.

IAN. I used to get rent.

JEANNIE. Is it because of the mask?

IAN. No.

JEANNIE. You want to know why I go out with Zan?

IAN. Nah, it makes perfect sense. You're a good match.

JEANNIE. Wow.

IAN. You're attracted to his looks.

JEANNIE. Well, sure, but it's more / than

IAN. And he's attracted to yours. It's very shallow. But, if it works / for you –

JEANNIE. It's more than that.

IAN. No.

JEANNIE. Yes it is. How do you know? Yes it is so. It's his... manner. It's the way he...you know. I like the way he talks. And the way he moves. He has a sort of... charisma. He has this attitude like everything is ok – like it's all going to work out fine. I like that.

IAN. But it might not work out fine. Given his inability to attend to his most basic human needs, he may be completely mistaken. He may find that it's not all fine.

JEANNIE. Well, he gets by.

IAN. He's a user.

JEANNIE. Ian. I think if you have his optimism, that way of approaching the world, things will work out for you. I think that attitude of well-being brings well-being to you.

IAN. *(pauses the game for a moment to talk to her)* Our society considers him good looking, and so he's given things.

He doesn't have to work for what he gets. And he assumes he'll always be good looking, and he'll always be given an easy ride. That is what you find attractive. That is what draws you to him. That air of privilege. Call it optimism or whatever makes you feel good about your choice, but what you see in him is the cocky arrogance that comes with the easy ride. And you've clearly been on that same ride. So...great. Enjoy the ride together.

But...what happens if you get acid thrown in your face?

JEANNIE. What!?

IAN. Or you're disfigured in some other way. Or you get fat. Or you just age badly. What resources will you and Zander have to rely on then? You've blithely gone through life thinking you won't need to develop other strengths.

JEANNIE. I'm in school! I was at the top of my class in high school. I'm studying so that I could actually help someone. Help kids, kids who don't have anyone /to turn to.

IAN. *(sincere)* No. You're right.

JEANNIE. That's your fucked up thing – deciding that's all I'm about. That's you being shallow. That's not me, that's you.

IAN. No. You're right. That wasn't fair.

JEANNIE. Yeah.

(beat)

IAN. Chuck was there when you met Zan.

JEANNIE. Yeah?

IAN. And Chuck actually *is* smart and funny.

JEANNIE. No, I know. Totally.

IAN. Both Chuck and I were there. At the Radio Shack that day.

JEANNIE. Yeah. I remember.

(Pause. He goes back to playing.)

But it was Zander who talked to me.

IAN. Ok.

JEANNIE. I mean, it was Zander who was joking around. Remember? And then he asked me out.

IAN. Right.

JEANNIE. Any one of you could have asked me out.

IAN. Right.

JEANNIE. But it was Zan. Who did.

IAN. Ok.

(pause)

But now it's several months later.

JEANNIE. Yeah?

IAN. And you actually know him.

JEANNIE. Yes.

IAN. And you're still with him.

JEANNIE. Yeah…

(They both just sit for a moment.)

Guess I should really go study.

IAN. Yup.

(pause)

JEANNIE. You would rather I didn't come around here… unless Zan is here?

(He says nothing.)

K. That's cool.

IAN. No.

(pause)

JEANNIE. No, it's not cool or…no you wouldn't rather?

(He says nothing.)

Do you mind? If I'm here? When Zan isn't here?

IAN. No.

JEANNIE. Oh. Ok. Ok. See you.

IAN. Yes.

JEANNIE. When Zan gets in could you tell him…

(He puts his headset back on.)

Ok. See you later Ian.

(She leaves.)

Scene Five

(**CHUCK** and **ZAN** and **JEANNIE** are playing with Xbox controllers.)

ZANDER. Ok, dudes. After this battle I've really got to go.

JEANNIE. Yeah, babe? I'm coming too, right?

ZANDER. You're the sweetest, babe.

CHUCK. I thought I was the sweetest.

JEANNIE. I'm really proud of you, babe. You're so close.

ZANDER. Thanks. Yeah. After Karen, one more recruit, and I'm golden. I think maybe Amy…

CHUCK. I'm proud of you too, babe.

ZANDER. Then you can be the first to buy some product.

CHUCK. Oh shit.

ZANDER. I'll do a whole workup on you. I'll shoot in some numbers and come up with the exact supplements and nutrients to fit your needs.

CHUCK. I'm aiming for perfectly perfect in every way. I'll take a bottle of that.

ZANDER. Let's work on some modest goals to start Chuckstein. Like, let's make you smell less.

(They all react to something on the screen. Big celebration!)

ALL. Woohoo! Yes!

JEANNIE. We did it? Right? We broke through? Is this… Is this it?

CHUCK. Now we must storm the castle!

ZANDER. Laterz. I mean, you guys can keep playing games if you want, but, you know, I'm about changing my life and the lives of all I encounter so….

JEANNIE. But I'm coming with, right?

ZANDER. Nah, babe. That's cool. Why don't you just stay here and wait for my triumphant return.

JEANNIE. But I told Karen I'd come by. I think she's expecting….

(He stops her with a kiss, and then runs up the stairs.)

ZANDER. Be back in an hour! Love ya!

JEANNIE. Oh. Ok! Bye, hon. Love ya.

(She stands uncertainly. He's just disappeared on her again.)

CHUCK. You wanna keep playing?

JEANNIE. Nah. Let's wait for Z to storm the castle or whatever.

CHUCK. K.

JEANNIE. Ya.

(awkward)

CHUCK. You feel like fixing up Daphne's pad?

JEANNIE. I should really go study.

CHUCK. Come on. You're not going to just leave her homeless. I mean, she's welcome to bunk with Earl, but they might want a change of scenery now and then.

JEANNIE. I dunno, Chuck. It just feels a little weird.

CHUCK. What?

JEANNIE. We kinda.. I think we…crossed a line. Don't you?

CHUCK. No.

JEANNIE. I just felt a little weird after. Didn't you?

CHUCK. I felt like I needed some "alone time." *(laughs)* Hey, it's just play.

JEANNIE. I know.

CHUCK. I mean, they're characters. It's not as if we're really doing anything.

JEANNIE. No, I know.

CHUCK. It was fun, right? Wasn't it fun?

JEANNIE. It was, but I just felt like…

CHUCK. What?

JEANNIE. Like.. Would we have played the same if Zan had been in the room?

CHUCK. Sure. He does role-play shit too. We should do it with him too some time. I mean, / we could all…

JEANNIE. You would have really done, or Earl would have done all that, with Daphne, if Zan had been watching?

CHUCK. I don't know. Maybe not. I don't know.

JEANNIE. Yeah.

CHUCK. Then, let's just fix up your place. Get you some furniture.

JEANNIE. Yeah?

CHUCK. Earl can be Daphne's moving man.

JEANNIE. Ok!

(*She sits with him and he fires it up.*)

CHUCK. I've given you another 500 credits.

JEANNIE. I can't keep taking your money.

CHUCK. Once Daphne gets a job she can pay Earl back.

JEANNIE. (*laughing*) A job? Oh my God. What will Daphne do?

CHUCK. Well, we'll have to see what she's good at.

(*She laughs.*)

You like this couch?

JEANNIE. No.

CHUCK. Ok. Tell me when.

JEANNIE. No. No. Hey! That's like my friend Sandy's couch. In life.

CHUCK. Cool. Where should I put it?

JEANNIE. Put it against that wall.

CHUCK. Yes ma'am.

JEANNIE. Move it down just a little. A little closer to the window.

CHUCK. I like it when you order me around.
      Why don't you sit on it and see if it's to your liking. We can exchange it if it's too…

JEANNIE. No. It's great.

CHUCK. Cool. What next? Coffee table... Pictures... Entertainment center...

JEANNIE. Why don't you sit too? See what you think?

CHUCK. Ok.

JEANNIE. Good?

CHUCK. Move down a little. I want to see if I could stretch out on it. You know, if Earl and Daphne have a late night playing canasta or something, and he decides to stay over – he wouldn't want to disturb her in the bedroom.

JEANNIE. Fine fine. Lie down. It's the perfect length.

CHUCK. That's what she said.

(**JEANNIE** *laughs and gives him a swat. He laughs and shoves her back.*)

(*She types something. He just looks at the screen for a moment. Thinks about it. Then types something back. They begin madly typing again. And then moving their characters.*)

(*They are getting very engrossed again, and clearly crossing the line* **JEANNIE** *had been concerned about.*)

(**IAN** *comes in, exhausted, goes directly to his screen and fires it up.*)

(*They both freeze. Their characters are in compromising positions.*)

IAN. *(in sullen greeting)* Peoples.

CHUCK. E! Hey! You just getting in man?

JEANNIE. Hi Ian.

IAN. Ya.

(*He begins playing.*)

JEANNIE. *(quietly to* **CHUCK***)* Get off me.

CHUCK. Huh?

JEANNIE. Off. Daphne.

CHUCK. Oh! Sorry.

(He moves his character.)

JEANNIE. I should really go study.

CHUCK. You okay, E?

IAN. Kinda burnt.

CHUCK. How was it today? Were you flying again?

IAN. Finished my 30 hours. Which sucks. It was awesome. The flying. The real flying.

CHUCK. You're done already?

IAN. I'm doing three month's of training in three weeks.

CHUCK. Holy shit.

JEANNIE. You're just coming in…from yesterday?

(IAN nods.)

Morning?

CHUCK. Holy shit, dude.

JEANNIE. That's not healthy.

IAN. You think?

JEANNIE. You should go sleep.

IAN. It's cool. They're understaffed. Guy who had me up in the plane hadn't slept in like two days. It's just the way it is.

JEANNIE. How scary. My dad said…

(They all decide to ignore this.)

CHUCK. So now you're ready? For real combat?

IAN. I can neither confirm nor deny.

(another awkward pause)

CHUCK. We were just outfitting Jeannie's E-Chuck City pad.

IAN. Yeah. I noticed.

CHUCK. Want to join us?

JEANNIE. I should really go study.

IAN. Sure. Why not.

CHUCK. Wow! Ok! Cool.

IAN. None of my guys are on anyway.

CHUCK. Great. *(to JEANNIE)* Ian is Captain Outstando.

JEANNIE. *(laughs)* Awesome. I'm Daphne. Or…she is.

(He joins them – brings his character in.)

Hah. Hello Captain Outstando. He's cute.

IAN. You go for leotards?

JEANNIE. I like the cape.

CHUCK. I'm going to show you some tables, lamps, chairs – get the place cozy.

IAN. Here's a couple thousand credits.

JEANNIE. No! Don't! I'll get a job.

IAN. I never play this anymore. You may as well have them.

CHUCK. Awesome. You should get like a grand piano for this room. And a real swag entertainment center.

JEANNIE. Guys. I wouldn't live this way if I won the lottery.

CHUCK. Daphne goes for the nice things in life.

(They type a few things to each other.)

JEANNIE. How do I… I want to offer you lemonade. How do I…

CHUCK. Lemonade! Daphne needs a liquor cabinet!

IAN. Here. Walk through here and we'll set up a kitchen.

(He takes her keyboard, and starts madly ordering her things.)

JEANNIE. I love that! Yellow, ok? Nice. No – I want a breakfast nook!

(He does it.)

With bar stools!

IAN. Done. Here's your fridge. Stocked with… *(He clicks the controller.)* lemonade.

JEANNIE. Wow. That's awesome. Ok. You fellas go to the living room and I'll bring you some refreshments.

CHUCK. Yes, ma'am.

(They all move their characters.)

JEANNIE. I'll put yours here. On this very cute end table.

IAN. I'll take the couch.

CHUCK. Could you set up at least a CD player, E. I want to put on some music.

(*IAN does. We hear music coming from the screen.*)

JEANNIE. I love this!

(*They all settle in and type and move for a few moments.* **JEANNIE** *types.* **IAN** *types.* **CHUCK** *types.* **JEANNIE** *laughs. She types.* **IAN** *types something. Both* **CHUCK** *and* **JEANNIE** *look at him.* **CHUCK** *types something back.* **IAN** *types again.* **IAN** *moves his character.*)

CHUCK. What are you doing man?

(**JEANNIE** *is just paralyzed.*)

IAN. What?

CHUCK. Don't do that.

IAN. That's not ok? I thought that was ok. That's not ok, Jeannie?

CHUCK. Cut it out, Ian.

IAN. You don't like that? Or... Daphne doesn't? It seemed like she does.

(**JEANNIE** *stands up. She doesn't know what to say. She just heads up the stairs. We hear the front door shut.*)

CHUCK. What the fuck?

(**IAN** *gets up and exits to the back room.*)

Scene Six

(IAN is alone, playing a war game with an online friend. He wears his headset. We can vaguely hear shouting and gunfire and explosions.)

IAN. Look out – there's someone behind that Humvee!

(His friend nails the guy.)

Oh, dude! Awesome! He didn't see you coming!

(They enjoy this together. We hear chatter over the lines.)

Oh crap. We're surrounded. We're going to need more backup... Wasn't Titan 27 gonna meet us here? Where are Mongo and Bullet 6? They were supposed to be in this. What the hell, right? If you say you're gonna show up, show up.

Shit. There's too many of them. I don't think we can take 'em alone.

Ahhh! Frag out! I'm going to detonate!

(explosion)

Awesome! Ok. Cool. You lead.

(a beat while they move to another location)

So listen, dude. You ever wonder, what if this thing was real?

Yeah, but I mean like...what if those were actual people we were blowing up and shit, you know?

Hah! Right! Get those bastards! Totally.

(Something happens on screen. IAN screws up.)

Oh. Shit. Sorry dude.

Yeah, I'm a little slow tonight. I... I didn't get much sleep.

Right?

(beat)

But, what if it weren't soldiers. That you hit. What if...

No, I know. Collateral damage. Absolutely.

(We hear the guy on the other end barking orders faintly.)

Good one!

(He plays.)

But, listen, dude. Listen. What if you've got this…this building in your crosshairs, you've been watching it, you know they're keeping weapons in there, you've done your surveillance. You've…you've done your job. You know it's a good target. You get the order, you fire, and just before the missile hits, like two seconds, this kid, this little girl, looks to be Addie's age – your sister's age, this…this kid walks around the shed. Out of nowhere. This little girl…

(Something awful happens on the screen. **IAN** *covers his face which makes them crash. He is shaken, breathing hard. He comes back in.)*

Ah! Oh fuck man. I'm sorry.

(Pause. He is very shaken.)

Wow, I'm really off tonight. Sorry.
Yeah.

(beat)

Hey, where are you dude?
Hah. Yeah. No, I mean, I.R.L. Where do you live? I'm in Nevada, are you…
Oh. Yeah? No. That's cool. Totally. I should really go too, my buddy just got here.
Ok, dude. See you later.

(He logs out. And just sits in the darkened room alone as lights fade.)

Scene Seven

(CHUCK is alone, playing. Probably a fantasy game. Maybe the sound of a monster on screen.)

(ZANDER comes in, wild eyed.)

ZANDER. Chuck. God. Is Jeannie here?

CHUCK. No. I haven't seen her in a like a week, dude. Did she tell you – it was a little weird, last / time she was here….

ZANDER. You got to help me out. I don't know… I don't know what I'm supposed to do here.

CHUCK. What happened? You ok?

ZANDER. I went to get the product. To the.. Proneutra /

CHUCK. Yeah?

ZANDER. Headquarters…or whatever.

CHUCK. Yeah.

ZANDER. And it's gone.

CHUCK. What do you mean? Did you have the right address?

ZANDER. Yeah, I had the fucking address. The building is fucking there. But… It's empty.

CHUCK. Oh shit.

ZANDER. They cleared out.

CHUCK. Oh shit, man.

ZANDER. I gave them the money. I gave them the money from the five kids I got to sign on.

CHUCK. Fuck.

ZANDER. I'd given it to them. Jeannie too. I mean, I got Jeannie in on this.

CHUCK. Yeah. Wow.

ZANDER. And…they're gone.

CHUCK. You gotta call the cops man.

ZANDER. Yeah?

CHUCK. You gotta…the better business bureau or…

ZANDER. Do you think there's any way…

CHUCK. What?

ZANDER. Do you think there's any way it could just be…
like a mix-up? Like, maybe they moved or… I don't
know…

CHUCK. Dude. You were rooked. There's like… It was a
fantasy dude. It was a con.

ZANDER. Fuck.

(He sits down and starts playing during this.)

CHUCK. Yeah.

ZANDER. Fuck.

CHUCK. I'm sorry, dude.

ZANDER. Yeah. Oh fuck. I have to tell all those kids…
Jeannie.

CHUCK. Yeah.

ZANDER. Shit, man. I should just move. I should just…find
a place I can…

CHUCK. Call the cops. You gotta report this.

ZANDER. You think maybe they'll catch them? Get the
money back?

CHUCK. No.

ZANDER. Shit.

CHUCK. But, who knows right? Maybe, right?

ZANDER. Fuck.

CHUCK. Yeah.

ZANDER. God, Chuck. What do I do? God.

CHUCK. Well, first you call, before you even tell /any of
the…

ZANDER. No. What do I DO? I mean, what do I do? My life?!

CHUCK. Yeah.

ZANDER. I've got like… I don't know.

CHUCK. You could try to go for training again – for dealing.
You could try craps this time. Or bartending.

ZANDER. Yeah. I'd have to find a different school.

CHUCK. You would have to show up. Every class this time.

ZANDER. And I'm broke. Totally broke.

CHUCK. Yeah.

ZANDER. I mean, I'm way beyond broke.

CHUCK. Sorry, dude. Really.

ZANDER. I couldn't even swing the cost of the class. Do you think maybe Ian would…

CHUCK. No, dude. I don't think so.

ZANDER. Yeah. I can't believe it. Those guys were so… I mean it was an awesome product.

CHUCK. Yeah.

ZANDER. And the whole thing…it seemed so…

CHUCK. Yeah.

ZANDER. It was such a great business. I can't believe this.

CHUCK. Wasn't real, man.

ZANDER. Shit. What do I do?

(They are silent for a moment.)

CHUCK. Go to the police station. File a report.

ZANDER. Yeah. Maybe they'll catch them…

(He finishes his round for a moment. Gets up to go.)

If Jeannie comes by, tell her…well, just…you know what, let me tell her, ok?

CHUCK. Good.

*(**ZAN** stands at the bottom of the stairs for a long moment. Not moving.)*

You want me to come with you dude?

ZANDER. Would you?

CHUCK. Sure. One sec.

*(He finishes something on the screen, and then joins **ZAN**. They exit.)*

Scene Eight

(IAN is in his chair, playing a war game. We hear the crashes and screams and artillery fire and bombs that accompany it. He puts on a headset. It's different from the one he usually wears to play. It's his work headset.)

(The sound goes off from the video game and the lighting shifts so we only see IAN in his chair. IAN at work. We hear voiceovers of the men IAN hears over his headsets, including the pilot who sits to the left of him. The voiceovers are confusing and sometimes overlap.)

VO1. Roger received target / 15.

VO2. See all those people standing down / there?

VO1. Stay firm. And open the courtyard.

VO.3. *(IAN's pilot)* Pull back. Wide shot.

(IAN does this.)

Yeah roger. I estimate there's probably about 20 / of them.

VO4. Hey Bushmaster element. Copy on / the one-six.

VO3. That's a weapon.

VO1. Hotel two-six; crazy horse / one eight.

VO3. Bushmaster six-romeo. / Roger.

VO1. Fucking / prick.

VO3. Hotel Two-six. This is crazy horse one-eight. Have individuals with weapons.

IAN. Is that a weapon? Sir? / It looks like…

VO1. He's got a weapon too. Hotel Two-Six, Crazy Horse / one-eight.

VO3. Have five to six individuals with AK 47s. Request permission to / engage.

IAN. Those aren't… Sir, no confirmation on the AK /47's, sir.

VO2. Roger that. We have no personnel east of our position. So you are free to engage. / Over.

VO3. All right. We'll be engaging.

VO2. Roger. / Go ahead.

IAN. We can't get 'em now because they're behind that building. / Sir.

VO1. He's got an RPG!

IAN. That may be a camera, sir. That the guy in the / front...

VO3. All right, we got a guy with an RPG. I'm gonna fire.

VO1. Hotel Two-Six; have eyes on individual with RPG. Getting ready to fire. / We won't...

VO2. Yeah. - and now he's behind the building. God / damn it.

VO3. Uh, negative, he was, uh, right in front of the Brad. Uh, 'bout there, /one o'clock.

IAN. I didn't... I can't ID that...that /weapon.

VO2. Just fuckin', once you get on 'em /deploy.

VO3. All /right.

VO1. I see your element, got about four Humvees /out along...

VO2. You're /clear...

IAN. What is he carrying? Sir. Permission to... /That's not...

VO3. All right, preparing to deploy.

(This is to **IAN***:)*

S.O. Prepare to target.

IAN. Yes Sir.

VO1. Let me know when you've /got 'em.

VO3. And... Sensor, on target!

IAN. Roger. On target.

VO3. Currently engaging approximately 8 indivuals, uh KIA, RPGs, and Ak-47s.

VO2. Hotel... Bushmaster Two-Six. We need to move, time now!

(There is the sound of an enormous explosion. **IAN** *covers his face as if it's happening in the room.)*

VO1. Yeah, we see 2 birds and they're still on fire.

VO3. Roger. I got em.

*(***IAN*** *is now staring at the screen, heart pounding, out of breath.)*

VO1. Two-six, this is two-six, we're / mobile.

VO2. Oops. I'm sorry. What was / going on?

VO3. God damit it, Kyle. All right, / I hit'em

VO1. All right. You're / clear.

VO4. Bushmaster Six; this is Bushmaster 2-6. Got a bunch of bodies layin' / there.

VO2. Yeah, we got one guy crawling around down there. But, uh, you know, /we got, definitely got…

VO1. We're shooting some /more.

VO2. Roger. Hey, you shoot, / I'll talk.

VO1. Hotel 2-6; you need to move that location once crazyhorse is done and get pictures over. Sargeant Twenty is the / location.

VO3. Pull in closer S.O. We need a body count.

(but **IAN** *is frozen)*

VO2. Hotel Two-six; crazyhorse one-eight. Can we get a confirmation on that body count?

VO3. *(firmly, to* **IAN**.*)* Pull in S.O. Now!

*(***IAN*** *is frozen.)*

Now S.O!

IAN. *(snapped out of his stupor)* Sir!

VO1. Crazyhorse one-eight; this is hotel 2-6 / over.

VO3. Oh, yeah. Look at those dead / bastards.

VO1. Nice.

VO2. Good shoot'n

VO3. Thank you. *(to* **IAN***)* Good shootin' S.O.

IAN. *(completely shaken and staring at the screen)* Thanks.

VO4. Crazyhorse One-8; Bushmaster Seven. / Go ahead.

VO3. Location of bodies.

IAN. *(checking the map which is over the live feed)* Mike bravo 5-4-5-8-8-6-1-7

VO3. Hey good on / the uh…

VO1. Mike bravo 5-4-5-8-8-6-1-7 over.

VO3. This is Crazyhorse One-8. That's a good copy.

*(to **IAN**)* Good work.

IAN. Thank you sir.

(He takes off his headset and the lights shift. Once again we hear the sounds of the war game and he has his controller in his hands.)

(He looks around stunned, disoriented, out of breath, panting. Unsure where he is. There is an explosion on the screen. He jumps.)

*(We hear the door upstairs. **IAN** is very startled. Shaken. We hear **JEANNIE**'s voice.)*

JEANNIE. Zan?

(There is a pause. She is uncertain whether to come down. But she starts down the steps.)

Zander?

*(She sees **IAN** and stops half way down the stairs.)*

Guess he's not here. Ok. Sorry.

(Stands for a moment. Decides to come down.)

I guess we should talk about…what happened.

*(**IAN** bends in half and holds his head as if it is aching. His eyes closed.)*

Look, it was fucked up, what Chuck and I were doing. I know. It's just a game, but… So, I don't blame you for judging me. Really. I'm not gonna do it any more.

(He does not respond. She comes into the room.)

Are you ok?

(He doesn't respond. She goes to him.)

Ian?

You must be exhausted.

(IAN still has his head in his hands but he grasps his hair in fists as if he is holding himself together.)

Look, this job – I'm sure you're great at it, but it's not worth it. It's not healthy. And you could do anything. I mean, you're smart and capable and...

(She goes to him tempted to stroke his hair. Stops herself. He is coiled. Taut.)

I can't imagine what you've seen. So awful. And even if it is, you know, the "bad guys", if there are "bad guys" – to have to kill them... I mean, they have lives too – mothers and girlfriends and sisters...

(He moans slightly. She is overcome with sympathy and reaches out cautiously. Strokes his hair.

(He springs up with a roar and grabs her hands before she can even scream. Holds them above her head. Pushes her back so she trips backward. Falling partially onto the couch.)

IAN. Shut up shut up / shut up shut up shut up shut up shut up!

JEANNIE. Ouch. Ian. Stop! What are you doing? Stop it!

(He pushes her down on the couch and pins her with his knee.)

JEANNIE. Don't do this. Why are you doing this?

IAN. I don't know!

JEANNIE. Stop it. You're hurting me.

IAN. Is this happening? IS IT?

JEANNIE. Let me go!

IAN. *(He lets her hands go.)* Fight me. Come on! Hit me! HIT ME!

(She smacks him hard and pushes him off her. He doesn't fight back. She knocks him back and he falls. She smacks him again.)

(not fighting) Again.

(She is about to hit him again. He makes no attempt to fight back. She begins crying.) Hit me! I can't feel it! Hit me again!

(ZAN and CHUCK have entered upstairs and hear them. Rushing down the stairs.)

ZANDER. What the fuck!?

(ZAN charges in with a roar and starts pounding IAN.)

You fucking bastard! What the hell were you doing?

(CHUCK tries to stop him.)

JEANNIE. Don't Zan. Stop. Stop it!

(IAN doesn't fight back, he just takes his pounding. He makes no sound.)

(CHUCK pulls ZAN off him. IAN is motionless on the floor.)

ZANDER. What did he do? I want to fucking KILL / him.

CHUCK. Jesus. What the / hell?

JEANNIE. Ian, are you ok?

ZANDER. What did he do to you?

(CHUCK goes to IAN and tries to help him up. IAN does not respond.)

CHUCK. Zan, help me out here. Let's get him to the couch.

IAN. *(in a dead toned voice)* No. Just go. I'm ok. Just…just get out of here.

ZANDER. Come on, Jeannie.

CHUCK. Do you need to like, go to the doctor?

IAN. No. Get out.

ZANDER. Fucking bastard.

JEANNIE. Just let him be.

ZANDER. Let him be? What the fuck?

*(He storms out. **JEANNIE** runs upstairs.)*

CHUCK. You okay, man?

IAN. I don't know.

*(**JEANNIE** comes back down with some ice in a cloth. Goes to **IAN**. Puts it on his head. He pushes it away. She sets it down.)*

IAN. Please, please just go.

CHUCK. Dude, you're bleeding.

IAN. I need… I'm sorry. I need you to go.

(They watch as he takes the ice, puts it on his bloodied head, and gets up, painfully. He goes to his chair and turns on the screen. We hear fireplay. They watch him playing as the lights fade.)

Scene Nine

(**IAN** *is at his screen, cleaned up a bit. He plays throughout this. His voice is expressionless.* **CHUCK** *is sitting on the couch watching* **ZAN** *pack things into his backpack – cables, controllers, even some beer and Ramen noodles.*)

ZANDER. I think this controller was mine.

CHUCK. No, dude.

ZANDER. I'm pretty sure I got it when we went to radio shack that time and we / got the cables for…

CHUCK. Ian bought them.

ZANDER. Yeah?

CHUCK. Ian bought the cables too.

ZANDER. Wow. I totally thought I / bought the…

IAN. Take them.

ZANDER. Yeah?

IAN. Take whatever you want.

ZANDER. You sure?

CHUCK. E-man.

IAN. I'm sure.

CHUCK. Ian, what the fuck. He just beat the shit out of you. I mean, what the fuck.

IAN. It's ok. I had it coming.

CHUCK. Did you? What did you do?

IAN. I don't know.

CHUCK. No really, what happened here?

IAN. I don't know, Chuck. Ok? I don't know what happened.

ZANDER. I'm sorry I went ballistic on you. I saw Jeannie crying…

IAN. No… You were right.

ZANDER. Ok.

(*He packs a bunch of things into his backpack.*)

CHUCK. You don't even have an Xbox. You don't even have a TV. You don't even have a place to live. What the hell do you need Ian's shit for?

ZANDER. I'll find a place.

CHUCK. Where?

ZANDER. I dunno. I'll just.. I'll let you know.

(He jams things into his backpack.)

CHUCK. Did you tell Jeannie?

ZANDER. Well…

CHUCK. Did you? Did you tell her anything? About the vitamins? About you / taking off?

ZANDER. I will. I'll let her know once I'm settled.

CHUCK. That is so fucked up, Z. That is totally fucked up.

ZANDER. I know.

CHUCK. She deserves way better. She / deserves…

ZANDER. I know.

CHUCK. So don't do it. Don't run out. Tell them all you fucked up. Find a way to pay them back. Come on.

ZANDER. I will. I'll totally pay everybody back. I will. I just have to find a place, like, make a new start, you know? Get myself situated. I might go back to my parents for just a little bit.

CHUCK. What? Aw, dude!

ZANDER. Just till I get my shit together. Come on Chuck. I'm not gonna stay there.

CHUCK. You are. You're gonna have your mom doing your laundry when you're ancient. You're gonna be 35 and like – mom, where's my favorite Scuby-doo t-shirt?

ZANDER. Shut up.

(He's filled the bag. Hard to actually say goodbye.)

Ok, guys. I guess… I'm off.

CHUCK. Asshole.

*(ZAN and **CHUCK** chest bump and muss each other up a bit. It's tough for **CHUCK** to say goodbye. He'll probably never see him again. Sincerely:)*

Be well, dude. Grow up into a fine young man, ok?

ZANDER. I'll try.

*(He goes to **IAN**.)*

Bye, E.

IAN. *(still playing his game)* See ya.

ZANDER. I'll be sending you a check soon. Real soon.

IAN. Sounds good.

*(**ZANDER** leaves. **CHUCK** stands looking at **IAN**.)*

Scene Ten

(A couple of weeks have gone by. **IAN** *is alone at his screen. He plays, but with little animation.)*

(We hear the door open upstairs. **JEANNIE** *calls out.)*

JEANNIE. Hey!

*(***IAN*** hears her and stops playing. Needs to say something.)*

IAN. *(almost to himself)* Jeannie.

(She comes to the top of the stairs, tentatively, and sees him. She's carrying a backpack.)

JEANNIE. Oh. Ian. Hey.

(He looks up but still can't say anything.)

I'm just getting a couple things – I'd left some of my stuff. In Zan's room. So… I'm just gonna get those things. And…head out.

(no response)

Ok.

(She turns to head back out.)

IAN. Jeannie.

(She comes down a step.)

JEANNIE. Yeah?

IAN. *(It's hard for him to speak at all, and really hard to find the words here.)* I've wanted to say…

(pause)

JEANNIE. Yeah?

IAN. I've wanted to say…

(She comes halfway down the stairs.)

IAN. I don't… I don't know what happened. That day. That's not an excuse. There's no excuse. I just…

JEANNIE. Yeah.

(There's a pause. This sits between them.)

*(**CHUCK** comes in.)*

CHUCK. Jeannie?!

JEANNIE. Hey!

CHUCK. Oh wow. Jeannie! Hey! How've you been? Wow.

*(to **IAN**)* Jeannie!

JEANNIE. Sorry. I just came to get a few things I'd left in Zan's room.

CHUCK. Sure. Of course.

JEANNIE. And then I'll be…out of your hair.

CHUCK. You're not…in my hair. At all.

(beat)

JEANNIE. How've you been?

CHUCK. Ok. I guess. Hey, you're a graduate, huh?

JEANNIE. Yup. Last week.

CHUCK. Awesome! Congrats! Welcome to… Life!

JEANNIE. Thanks.

(They stand awkwardly for a moment.)

CHUCK. So…look at you. You're all grown up!

(She laughs.)

JEANNIE. Yeah.

(beat)

CHUCK. I guess…you heard from Zan, huh?

JEANNIE. He finally answered after like, 50 calls.

CHUCK. Wow.

JEANNIE. Yeah.

CHUCK. It was totally fucked up he didn't say goodbye or anything. Sorry.

JEANNIE. Yeah.

CHUCK. He just freaked about having to break it to everyone. I told him – man up dude. Just do it. But… / yeah.

JEANNIE. I had to tell everybody. That sucked.

CHUCK. Sorry.

JEANNIE. Karen was here on a scholarship. She has like, no money. Her parents were so pissed.

CHUCK. Yeah.

JEANNIE. Five hundred dollars.

CHUCK. Yeah.

JEANNIE. Guess we were all pretty stupid.

CHUCK. Nah. It seemed like a good thing.

JEANNIE. No, it didn't.

CHUCK. Yeah. No, it didn't.

(They chuckle.)

JEANNIE. Zan's a good salesman.

CHUCK. He is.

(pause)

JEANNIE. I got a job. At a daycare.

CHUCK. Cool. Good for you!

JEANNIE. Real life. We'll see how I do.

CHUCK. Right?

(JEANNIE sits on the couch.)

JEANNIE. I guess I should get my things. I left a few things. In Zan's room.

CHUCK. You can still come around. You know, to…hang out. Play some games.

JEANNIE. Yeah…

CHUCK. – you're really getting good on Hafadai. Level three battle gnome!

JEANNIE. Yeah. I think I'm kind of done with that.

CHUCK. Yeah? Ok. We still need to get Daphne a job.

JEANNIE. I think I'll see how Jeannie does with a job first.

CHUCK. Right.

JEANNIE. You keep Daphne. Get her some nice thigh-high spiky boots and a riding crop.

CHUCK. Done and done.

(a moment)

JEANNIE. I should really go.

(She continues not to.)

CHUCK. So, I won't see you online?

JEANNIE. Nah. I don't have any of that…stuff.

CHUCK. Right.

JEANNIE. Yeah.

CHUCK. Well, we'll always have Facebook.

JEANNIE. Right.

(They laugh a little grimly. She gets up heads to the stairs.)

Ok. Well, good to see you. Both of you. Take care of yourselves.

CHUCK. Hey.

JEANNIE. Yeah?

CHUCK. How would you like to grab a bite?

JEANNIE. You mean…food?

CHUCK. Yeah.

JEANNIE. Real food?

CHUCK. Why not?

JEANNIE. Out there?

CHUCK. I dunno. It was just a thought.

JEANNIE. How will we chat without the little box?

CHUCK. We could text each other. At the table.

(She hesitates for a long moment.)

Or some other time…

JEANNIE. I could use a burger.

CHUCK. Yeah?

JEANNIE. Yeah.

CHUCK. Awesome! That's totally…that's just awesome! Yes!

JEANNIE. *(laughing)* Cool. Let's go!

(He starts to head out with her and then stops. Looks at **IAN**. *He doesn't want to leave him alone.)*

Come on, Ian. You're coming too.

IAN. Nah.

CHUCK. Come on E-man.

IAN. No thanks.

(beat)

CHUCK. Dude, you haven't left this room in two weeks. It's time.

JEANNIE. You're coming with us.

(She steps toward him. Holds her ground. Very clearly to **IAN**.*)*

I'm only going to go if you come.

CHUCK. Dude!

*(***IAN*** *thinks a moment. Decides to help out his buddy. He finishes whatever was happening on screen. It takes a few moments. Closes it out. Goes to them. They all climb the stairs.* **CHUCK** *takes up the rear with a silent celebration. At the top they turn out the lights.)*